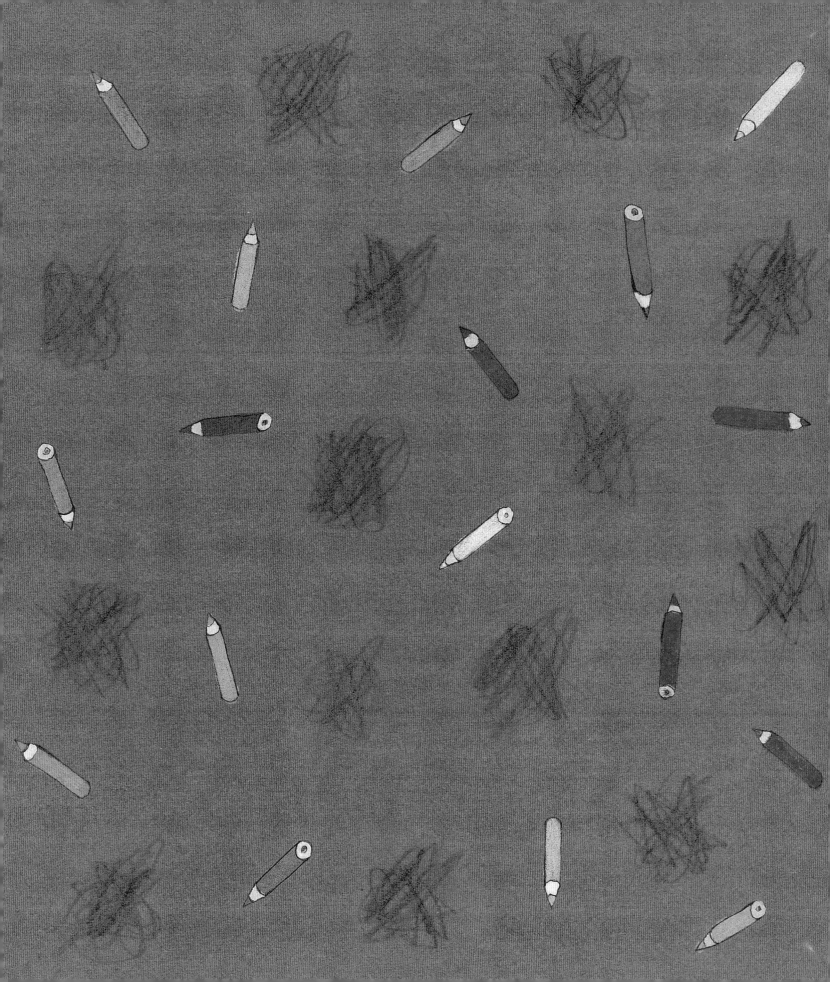

First published in 2010 by Child's Play (International) Ltd
Ashworth Road, Bridgemead, Swindon SN5 7YD

Distributed in USA by Child's Play Inc
250 Minot Avenue, Auburn, Maine 04210

Distributed in Australia by Child's Play Australia Pty Ltd
Unit 10/20 Narabang Way
Belrose, NSW 2085

Text and illustrations copyright © Hannah Cumming 2010
The moral right of the author/illustrator has been asserted

ISBN 978-1-84643-343-6
CLP080310CPL05103436

Printed and bound in Shenzhen, China

1 3 5 7 9 10 8 6 4 2

A catalogue record of this book is available from the British Library

www.childs-play.com

The Cloud

by Hannah Cumming

Child's Play®

Art Class was fun.
You could draw anything you wanted.

Everyone enjoyed it.

Well, almost everyone.

One girl sat by herself

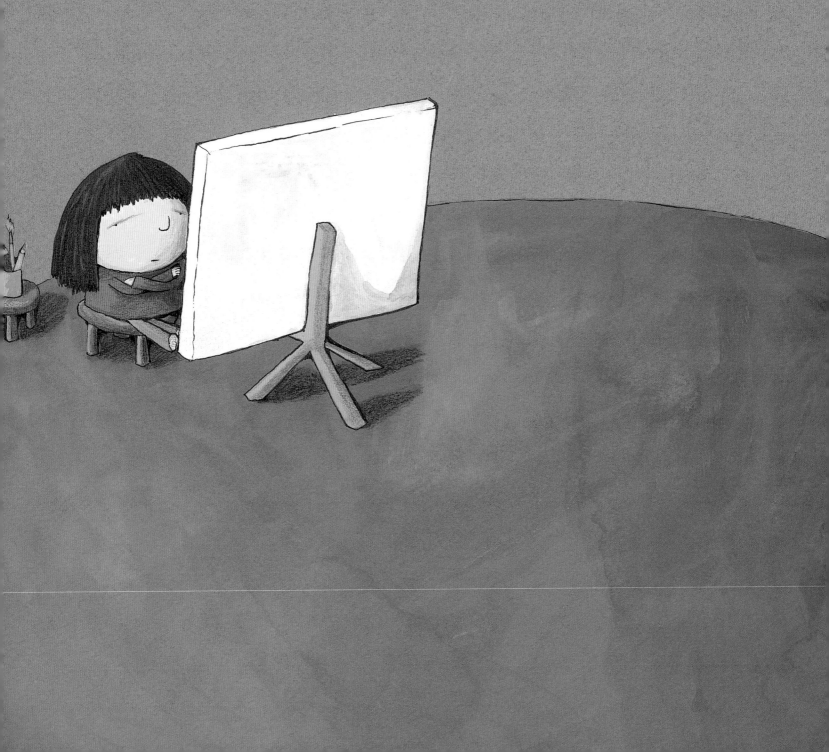

and drew nothing.

She seemed to have
a little black cloud above her.

No one spoke to her.

But one girl wanted to be friends.

Perhaps there was a way
through the black cloud.

She went over to chat,

but it didn't seem to work.

What else could she try?

Maybe...

...a drawing?

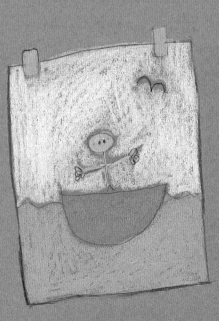

They could work
on it together!

It didn't seem to turn out very well.

But she was not going to give up...

...and after many attempts...

...there was a smile.

The other children had noticed
and thought it looked like a good game.

Before long, everyone was drawing together.

And the cloud was gone. Well, sort of!